ISBN 0-312-01067-2

First Edition

10 9 8 7 6 5 4 3 2 1

Messy Jessie

by Robie H. Harris
ILLUStrated by
Nicole Hollander

St. Martin's Press
New York

Jessie drew a big red circle . . . so big that it went right
off the paper and onto the table.
Jessie grinned.

She made big red dots on her hands.
She put big red dots all over her face and giggled
with delight!

"Oh no!" groaned Jessie's father.

He wiped Jessie's giant red circle off the table.

Jessie watched her circle disappear and scowled.

When her father tried to wipe the dots off her face,
Jessie howled.

Jessie's father gave her a cup of raspberry yogurt.
Jessie tipped the cup upside down and drew giant circles
in the smooth pink yogurt with her thumbs.

"Oh no! Another mess!" grumbled her father.

He wiped off the table and Jessie licked off her thumbs.
"How 'bout a carrot, my Messy Jessie?" her father asked.
Jessie smiled.
She liked it when her father called her Messy Jessie.

Jessie's father lifted her out of her highchair.

He opened the refrigerator and handed her a carrot.

"Here, Jessie. A carrot's not messy!" he said as he ran to answer the door.

Jessie peered into the refrigerator as she chomped on the carrot.

She ran her fingers over the cold, smooth eggs, picked
up one, and dropped it on the floor.
She liked watching the egg ooze along the floor.

She dumped out the milk, and some catsup . . .
and some mustard too.

She stepped into the eggs, the milk, the catsup, and the mustard.

She liked the feel of the cold wet mess on the bottom of her feet.

"Messy Jessie! Messy Jessie!" she sang as she slipped and slid.

The cat and dog lapped up a bit of the mess.
Footprints and pawprints covered the floor.

Jessie's father came back and gasped, "Oh no!"
Jessie gasped, "Oh no!" too.
"This isn't funny!" said her father.

Jessie grabbed a towel and tried to clean up.
She and her father wiped up the mess together.

I Like those dots.

Her father put her in the tub and washed raspberry yogurt out of her hair.

Jessie helped wash the eggs, milk, mustard, and catsup off her feet.

Her father washed the bright red dots off her hands.

But he left the dots on her face. He kinda liked them.

Jessie's father gave her a big hug and kissed her
goodnight.

"No more messes . . ." he said. "I love you, my
Messy Jessie."

"No messes," said Jessie as she hugged her father and
closed her eyes.

But, that night, Jessie dreamed about big red circles and
big red dots . . . crunchy orange carrots, smooth
pink yogurt, slippery white milk, slimy yellow eggs,
mushy yellow mustard and gushy red catsup,
all mixed together,
in one big mess!

messy Jessie